This Little Tiger book belongs to:

For my wonderful Mam and Dad, with love – J G

To Daniel – T W

LITTLE TIGER PRESS
An imprint of Magi Publications
1 The Coda Centre
189 Munster Road, London SW6 6AW
www.littletigerpress.com

First published in Great Britain 2010
This edition published 2010
Text copyright © Magi Publications 2010
Illustrations copyright © Tim Warnes 2010
Tim Warnes has asserted his rights to be identified
as the illustrator of this work under the Copyright,
Designs and Patents Act, 1988
A CIP catalogue record for this book
is available from the British Library

ISBN 978-1-84895-084-9
Printed in China
LTP/1800/0047/0510
10 9 8 7 6 5 4 3 2 1

Silent Night

Juliet Groom   Tim Warnes

LITTLE TIGER PRESS
London

All the animals gather together,

Silent, harmonious, happy forever.

Sleep in heavenly peace.
All together in peace.

Silent night, holy night,
Lift your hearts in joy tonight.

Take joy in our world, in the mountains so tall,
The flowers, so tiny – take joy in them all.

Celebrate all that we share.
Each precious moment we share.

Silent night, holy night,
Angels sing of love's pure light.

Love that brings a smile to each face,
That brightens each day with its
beauty and grace.

Cherish those dear to your heart.
Keep them safe, safe in your heart.

Silent night, holy night,
All the world holds its breath tonight.

High above, a bright star gleams,
The world reborn in radiant beams.

Hope for all in the world.

Hope for our beautiful world.

You will LOVE these beautiful books from Little Tiger Press

Christmas With You
Julia Hubery
Victoria Ball

Catherine Rayner
Iris and Isaac

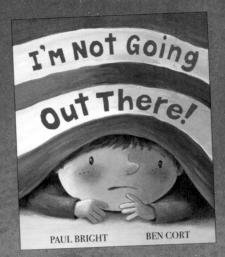

I'm Not Going Out There!
PAUL BRIGHT
BEN CORT

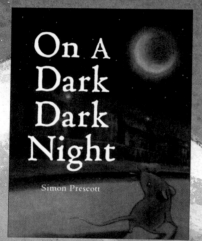

On A Dark Dark Night
Simon Prescott

There's No Such Thing As MONSTERS!
Steve Smallman
Caroline Pedler

I Love You as BIG as the World
David Van Buren
Tim Warnes

For information regarding any of the above titles
or for our catalogue, please contact us:
Little Tiger Press, 1 The Coda Centre,
189 Munster Road, London SW6 6AW
Tel: 020 7385 6333 • Fax: 020 7385 7333
E-mail: info@littletiger.co.uk • www.littletigerpress.com